Will Hobbs

My Favorite Writer

Megan Lappi

WEIGL PUBLISHERS INC.

Published by Weigl Publishers Inc.
350 5th Avenue, Suite 3304, PMB 6G
New York, NY 10118-0069

Web site: www.weigl.com
Copyright ©2007 WEIGL PUBLISHERS INC.
All rights reserved. No part of this publication may be reproduced,
stored in a retrieval system, or transmitted in any form or by any means,
electronic, mechanical, photocopying, recording, or otherwise, without
the prior written permission of Weigl Publishers Inc.

Library of Congress Cataloging-in-Publication Data

Lappi, Megan.
  Will Hobbs / Megan Lappi.
     p. cm. -- (My favorite writer)
  Includes bibliographical references and index.
  ISBN 1-59036-488-0 (lib. bdg. : alk. paper) -- ISBN 1-59036-489-9
(pbk. : alk. paper)
  1. Hobbs, Will--Juvenile literature. 2. Authors, American--20th century-
-Biography--Juvenile literature. 3. Children's stories--Authorship--
Juvenile literature. I. Title. II. Series.
  PS3558.O23Z76 2007
  813'.54--dc22
  [B]
                                            2006016106

Printed in the United States of America
1 2 3 4 5 6 7 8 9 0 09 08 07 06 05

Project Coordinator
Heather C. Hudak

Design
Terry Paulhus

All of the Internet URLs given in the book were valid at the time of
publication. However, due to the dynamic nature of the Internet, some
addresses may have changed, or sites may have ceased to exist since
publication. While the author and publisher regret any inconvenience this
may cause readers, no responsibility for any such changes can be accepted
by either the author or the publisher.

Contents

Will Hobbs

MILESTONES

1947 Born on August 22

1948 Boards a ship headed for Panama, along with his family

1969 Graduates with a bachelor's degree from Stanford University

1972 Marries Jean Loftus on December 20

1973 Moves with Jean to Colorado

1988 *Changes in Latitudes* is published

1990 Leaves teaching and becomes a full-time writer

1996 *Far North* is chosen as one of the top 10 titles of 1996 by the American Library Association

As a child, Will's family moved to new places all the time. His father was in the air force, and that meant the Hobbs family was never in one place for long. Because of this, books became Will's best friend. In a new place, with no friends, Will knew that he could always open up an adventure story and find old (and new) friends inside.

The outdoors and adventure were important to the Hobbs family. When he was not reading, Will spent much of his time outdoors with his brothers or his father. This helped the young boy appreciate nature and wildlife. Many of his **experiences** during this time made it into the pages of the novels Will wrote as an adult.

Although he was an **avid** reader, Will did not begin writing his own stories and poems until he was in college. Will was an English teacher for 17 years, and he shared his love of reading with his students. He still stays in touch with children he has met and taught. Will even writes stories based on ideas they provide.

Early Childhood

William Carl Hobbs was born on August 22, 1947, in Pittsburgh, Pennsylvania. His father, Gregory J. Hobbs, was a U.S. Air Force engineer. Will's mother, Mary Ann Rhodes Hobbs, was a homemaker.

Shortly after they were married, Mary and Gregory started their family. The first child to arrive was Greg Jr., followed next by Ed, and then by Will. When Will was 6 months old, he and his family moved to Panama. While in Panama, Will spent a great deal of time with his brothers. At age 2 or 3, Will ran at top speed to keep up with them. He joined in their rough games. Will later wrote about a boy who tries to find his two older brothers in the story *Jason's Gold.*

Gregory was an adventurous man. He wanted to show his wife and children the world. Will's mother also **inspired** Gregory to find new adventures.

More than 350,000 people live in Pittsburgh, Pennsylvania. It has a busy river port and is known as a center for education and technology.

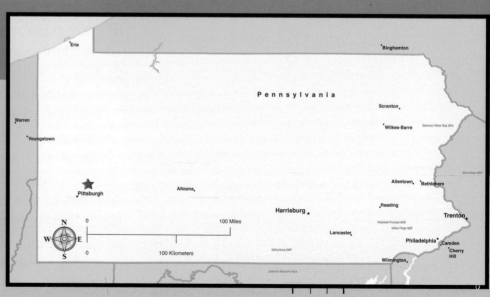

A few years later, the family moved again. They returned to the United States. Will started school in Falls Church, Virginia. It was the first of many schools Will would attend all across the United States. His family was close, and that made moving a little easier. Will also learned to make friends easily. Even though he had friends, reading remained important to him. Will spent many hours in the library reading every adventure book he could find.

The family's move to Alaska was especially important to Will. Will enjoyed the wilderness in Alaska. He loved the animals, the northern lights, and the history of the **Klondike Gold Rush**.

In Alaska, Will's father took the boys on many adventures. By this time, Will had a younger brother and sister, too. Will's father would take his sons out to fish in the Kenai River. Will remembers the sound of the river and the bear tracks they would find along the shore.

When the family moved away from Alaska, Will was very sad. He remembers sailing away from Alaska to California with tears in his eyes. However, Will knew he would return.

Will (left) played music with his siblings, Greg, Barbara, and Ed.

Growing Up

Will's love of animals began when he was just a child. When he was 4, Will and his two older brothers freed more than a dozen turtles from a neighbor's yard. Even then, Will believed it was not right to keep animals **captive**.

The three boys liked to catch animals and bring them home. However, Will's brothers always had a rule—all the animals they caught had to be returned to nature after four days. Will took this rule very seriously.

The Hobbs family moved to California when Will was in grade five. Will spent every day after school **exploring** the hills behind his house. After he had finished his paper route each day, Will headed outside to look for gopher snakes.

Will (left), Ed, and Greg enjoyed adventure.

Will also hiked on the weekends. He went on his first long **backpacking** trip when he was 12 years old. Will found many **artifacts** from the **pioneer** days at a place called Emigrant Gap. Artifacts made it into some of Will's later stories, including *Kokopelli's Flute*. In the story, a young boy is **transformed** into a packrat when he blows on an old flute that he finds in a cave.

In grade six, Will discovered that his teacher, Mr. Pilch, loved animals, too. Mr. Pilch was always looking for snakes to put in his **terrarium**. Will was happy to help. He would find a snake and bring it into Mr. Pilch's classroom to show the other students. After a few days, Will always released the snakes. He had learned something very important from his brothers.

Will did not always have good experiences with animals. Once, he and a cousin followed a skunk. They drew too near to the animal, and Will learned a good lesson. The smell of a skunk is difficult to remove.

Inspired to Write

Will writes about many different kinds of animals, but his favorite is probably the bear. Will fell in love with bears while he was living in Alaska. He says if he could be any land animal, he would want to be a grizzly bear.

Will loved to play games, including baseball.

When Will was about to enter high school, the Hobbs family moved to San Antonio, Texas. At Central Catholic High School, Will made new friends and soon found the school's library. Central prepared its students for college, and Will worked hard.

By his junior year, Will was the editor of the school's newspaper. It was an important experience for the young writer. Unfortunately, his father was soon **transferred** again—this time back to California. This time, Will did not move with his family. Instead, he spent the summer working at Philmont Scout Ranch in New Mexico.

The opportunity to work at Philmont was perfect for Will, and he jumped at the chance. Will had been a scout as a boy. His older brothers were also scouts. Will had worked hard to keep up with them. He had received many scout badges. In grade eight, Will proudly became an Eagle Scout.

Will and his niece Sarah have gone backpacking in Utah.

For the next three summers, Will worked at the camp. He began as a ranger and then became a camp director in the back country. In his spare time, he often went hiking. One of his older brothers, Greg, came along on many backpacking trips. One of their favorite hikes was the John Muir Trail along the Sierra Nevada.

At this time, Greg was studying at the University of Notre Dame in Indiana. Will also attended Notre Dame after he graduated from high school. Later, Will transferred to Stanford University near San Francisco.

At Stanford, Will studied American literature and began writing stories and poems. In 1969, Will graduated from Stanford with very high grades. He was offered a four-year **scholarship** to continue his studies. Will began school but lost interest. He decided to become a teacher after he met Jean Loftus, his future wife.

Will and his wife, Jean, enjoy spending time outdoors.

Favorite Books

When he was growing up, Will read as much as he could. He says, "I fell in love with stories." He loved stories so much that he would think about them all the time— even when he was not reading. Some of this favorite books were adventure stories, such as *Treasure Island* by Robert Louis Stevenson and *Tom Sawyer* by Mark Twain. He also liked reading about the latest adventures of the Hardy Boys.

Learning the Craft

Growing up, Will read all the time, but he did not write very much. He thought that good writers had to be very talented. He did not think that he had any talent. What he did not know at the time was that writers improve their skills with practice.

At first, Will wrote essays and book reports in school. As an ninth-grader at Central Catholic High School, Will read many books. His English teachers offered extra marks for writing book reports. So, after Will had finished reading a book from the library, he would write a book report.

In college, Will decided to write poems and stories. He became interested in reading about Native Americans, and he stayed home from school for a week to read The Lord of the Rings trilogy by J.R.R. Tolkien.

Will's biggest **breakthrough** as a writer came when he realized that if he could imagine himself as the characters in his stories, the stories came to life. It was as if the stories started to play out in his head. Will began writing down what he saw and what the characters were saying.

Will featured canyons he had visited in his book *The Maze.*

Many of Will's books began as images in his head. Before he wrote the story *Changes in Latitudes*, Will saw a picture of a sea turtle swimming in the ocean. He could not stop thinking about the turtle. He thought about the kinds of characters that would want to swim with the animal. It was not long before Will was using his imagination to create another story.

■ Will met with fans in Sitka, Alaska.

Getting Published

"By 1980, I couldn't stand not writing any longer and made myself sit down and work," Will wrote in an essay about his life. At this time, Will was working part time as a teacher. He was spending more and more time on his new career as a writer.

The first story he wrote was called *The Pride of the West*. Will worked on this story for 8 years. Publishers were not interested in *The Pride of the West*. Will **revised** his story five times and sent it to more publishers. Each time, however, he received a **rejection** letter.

Will was almost ready to give up when he decided to attend a writer's workshop in Aspen, Colorado. One of the writers there told him that rejection letters were a good sign. They meant that publishers were taking the time to write to Will. Many writers do not receive any responses. Will began to think that publishers liked his writing.

The Publishing Process

Publishing companies receive hundreds of **manuscripts** from authors each year. Only a few manuscripts become books. Publishers must be sure that a manuscript will sell many copies. As a result, publishers reject most of the manuscripts they receive.

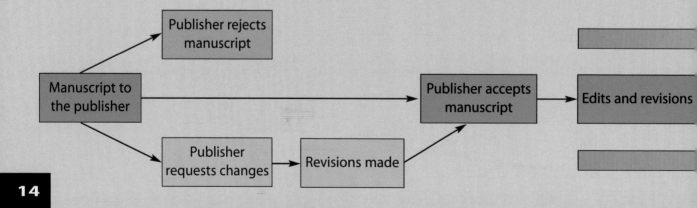

Will decided to try harder. While he was at the writer's workshop, he wrote a short story. The story later became the book *Changes in Latitudes*.

In 1988, *Changes in Latitudes* was published. After this book was published, Will re-sent the manuscript for *The Pride of the West*. In 1989, it was published, too, but under a new name—*Bearstone*. In 1990, Will stopped teaching and became a full-time writer.

Will takes about a year to write a new book. In that year, he spends about 6 months actually writing. The rest of the time he is traveling, speaking at conferences of teachers and librarians, spending time with his family, and going on wilderness adventures.

Inspired to Write

Getting ready to write is not easy for Will. He **procrastinates** for as long as possible. He even has a special deal he makes with a small toy. He winds it up, and when it has crossed the table, he knows it is time to start working. As soon as he starts writing, Will wonders why he waited so long. The characters come to life, and Will can hardly keep up with the stories as they appear on the page.

Once a manuscript has been accepted, it goes through many stages before it is published. Often, authors change their work to follow an editor's suggestions. Once the book is published, some authors receive royalties. This is money based on book sales.

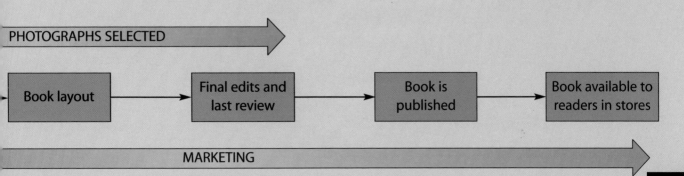

PHOTOGRAPHS SELECTED

Book layout → Final edits and last review → Book is published → Book available to readers in stores

MARKETING

Writer Today

By the time Will **devoted** his life to writing, he had already been a teacher for 17 years. He knew that he would miss the students in his classes, but he had learned what they liked to read. That made it much easier for him to write for his young audience.

Will and his wife, Jean, moved to southwestern Colorado in 1973, one year after they were married. They do not have any children of their own, but they do have many nieces and nephews.

Will spends as much time as he can outdoors, just as he did as a child. Will and Jean have been on many adventures. They hike in the San Juan Mountains and spend time on local rivers on board their whitewater raft.

The area around Will's home in Durango, Colorado, bursts with color in autumn.

Will says he has spent more than 6 months of his life on the Colorado River in the Grand Canyon. One of his biggest adventures has been rafting the Colorado River alone with his wife. "I had run those rapids before, but when you're down there alone, you're in a whole other dimension," he said.

In 2000, Jean and Will moved to a new home on the edge of Durango. Their house borders a large wildlife preserve. They can see all kinds of wildlife from their windows—elk, deer, eagles, bears, and mountain lions. For the boy who once loved wild animals so much, it is the perfect place to call home.

Will has rafted down the Colorado River in Arizona.

Popular Books

W ill has written 16 novels for young readers, as well as two picture books—*Beardream* and *Howling Hill*. Seven of his books were named Best Books for Young Adults by the American Library Association. They are *Bearstone, Downriver, The Big Wander, Beardance, Far North, The Maze,* and *Jason's Gold*. Will's favorite book is always the one he wrote most recently because the characters are still alive in his mind.

Bearstone

In 1979, a grizzly bear was killed in the San Juan Mountains in Colorado. It was an area where Will Hobbs often hiked. The bear's death gave Will the idea of writing about the last grizzly bear in Colorado.

Will created the story of 14-year-old Cloyd Atcitty. After running away from a group home for Native American boys, Cloyd is sent to live with a rancher named Walter. In a cave near the ranch, Cloyd discovers a turquoise bearstone. When Walter asks Cloyd to help him to re-open an old gold mine, Cloyd jumps at the chance. Out in the wilderness, Cloyd meets a grizzly bear. Soon, Cloyd tries to warn the bear about a hunter. He also must try to save Walter, who has been injured in a mining explosion.

AWARDS
Bearstone
1989 California Young Reader Medal

Changes in Latitudes
1992 Colorado Blue Spruce Young Adult Book Award

Beardance
1994 American Library Association Best Books for Young Adults award

Far North
1997 American Library Association Best Books for Young Adults award

Jason's Gold

Jason's Gold takes place in the past. It is set during the time of the Klondike Gold Rush. Some of the characters, such as writer Jack London, are based on real historical people. Will has said that the writing and research he did for *Jason's Gold* were among the most exciting things he has ever done.

The book begins with a boy named Jason Hawthorn heading north to find gold in the Klondike. On the way, he meets Jack, a Canadian girl named Jamie, and a dog he calls King. Together, they face moose, bears, and a very cold winter.

Will dedicated the book to his two older brothers. In the story, Jason tries to catch up with his two older brothers, who left three days earlier. Will remembered trying to keep up with his brothers as a kid and wanted to dedicate the story to them.

Ghost Canoe

Kokopelli's Flute

Will's first fantasy novel was titled *Kokopelli's Flute*. He had always loved fantasy. Will got the idea for the story from a picture of a flute player that ancient people had carved into a rock thousands of years ago.

Kokopelli's Flute is the story of a 13-year-old boy named Tepary Jones. One night, Tep takes a hike to the ancient cliff dwellings near his house and finds robbers stealing artifacts from the site. The robbers leave something behind—a flute carved from an eagle bone. Although he knows he should not, Tep picks up and plays the flute. Suddenly, he finds himself trapped in the body of a packrat.

Ghost Canoe

Will was a fan of mystery stories as a child. When his readers asked him to write a mystery, he decided it would be a good idea. Will wanted to make *Ghost Canoe* as exciting as *Treasure Island*, which was one of his favorite books when he was growing up.

Ghost Canoe begins with a ship breaking up on the rocks at Cape Flattery. Everyone on board the boat is said to have been killed. However, 14-year-old Nathan MacAllister, the son of the lighthouse keeper, is not convinced. Strange footprints on the beach, a theft at the trading post, and sightings of a "hairy man" lead Nathan to believe someone survived.

Alone in the forest, Nathan finds a skeleton and a burial canoe used by the Makah Natives. Has he unlocked the mystery?

Downriver

Downriver is another award-winning example of how Will Hobbs uses his real-life adventures to find ideas for his stories. With his wife, Jean, Will has spent many days on the Colorado River. He knows the river well.

In *Downriver*, 15-year-old Jessie is sent to an outdoor education camp. One day, Jessie and six friends steal a raft and head down the Colorado River. It is a dangerous river, and the kids are in for more than they expected. Soon, helicopters are chasing them down the river.

Will anyone get hurt? Will the group self-destruct? This is an exciting adventure story that readers find hard to put down.

AWARDS
Downriver

1995 California Young Reader Medal

1997 Colorado Blue Spruce Young Adult Book Award

Creative Writing Tips

S ome authors begin writing when they are young. Others, like Will, do not begin until they are older. Will had many adventures when he was young. These adventures helped him to write great stories as an adult. Here are some tips to think about as you write.

Have Memorable Experiences

Will says that many of his stories are based on his own experiences. When Will was a child, his family often moved from place to place. That gave Will many memories to draw from when he was writing his first adventure stories.

Read All the Time

Will read all the time as a child. Reading helped him to recognize good writing. If you read often, you will learn what makes a well-written story and how to develop interesting characters.

Will works from his home office.

Create Great Characters

Before he begins writing a story, Will writes as much as he can about each of his characters. He writes about what they like, their clothes, and even how they would talk. The characters he writes about are based on people he has known in his life, including students he has taught.

Practice

Do not worry if your first stories are not very well-written. Like anything, the more you practice, the better you will become. Will has written many books, and he gets better all the time. He says that writing is like practicing an instrument. You only get better by doing it.

Write and Re-write

Will begins with a **draft** of the story. Then, he re-writes it many times before he is pleased with the result. He usually writes at least three drafts of any story. The first draft is a way to get an idea on paper. With each new draft, Will begins fresh. He uses only the ideas from the last draft.

Inspired to Write

Like any good writer, Will is always looking for ideas for his stories. His novel *The Big Wander* was based on the story of a man who disappeared in the canyons of the Escalante River in Utah. "Years later, the image of boy, burro, and dog adventuring in that canyon still stuck in mind," he said.

Will has visited an area of Colorado known as "The Window." The location is featured in his books *Bearstone* and *Beardance*.

Writing a Biography Review

A biography is an account of an individual's life that is written by another person. Some people's lives are very interesting. In school, you may be asked to write a biography review. The first thing to do when writing a biography review is to decide whom you would like to learn about. Your school library or community library will have a large selection of biographies from which to choose.

Are you interested in an author, a sports figure, an inventor, a movie star, or a president? Finding the right book is your first task. Whether you choose to write your review on a biography of Will Hobbs or another person, the task will be similar.

Begin your review by writing the title of the book, the author, and the person featured in the book. Then, start writing about the main events in the person's life. Include such things as where the person grew up and what his or her childhood was like. You will want to add details about the person's adult life, such as whether he or she married or had children.

Next, write about what you think makes this person special. What kinds of experiences influenced this individual? For instance, did he or she grow up in unusual circumstances? Was the person determined to accomplish a goal? Include any details that surprised you.

A concept web is a useful research tool. Use the concept web on the right to begin researching your biography review.

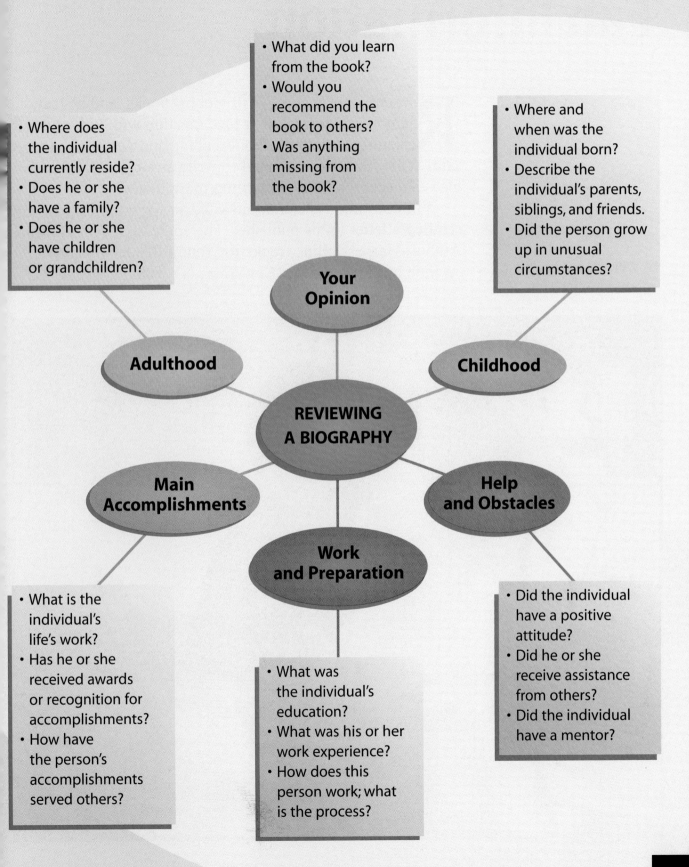

- Where does the individual currently reside?
- Does he or she have a family?
- Does he or she have children or grandchildren?

- What did you learn from the book?
- Would you recommend the book to others?
- Was anything missing from the book?

- Where and when was the individual born?
- Describe the individual's parents, siblings, and friends.
- Did the person grow up in unusual circumstances?

Your Opinion

Adulthood

Childhood

REVIEWING A BIOGRAPHY

Main Accomplishments

Help and Obstacles

Work and Preparation

- What is the individual's life's work?
- Has he or she received awards or recognition for accomplishments?
- How have the person's accomplishments served others?

- What was the individual's education?
- What was his or her work experience?
- How does this person work; what is the process?

- Did the individual have a positive attitude?
- Did he or she receive assistance from others?
- Did the individual have a mentor?

Fan Information

Readers love reading Will Hobbs' books, and he truly enjoys his fans, too. "I love meeting with kids and visiting with them about reading and writing," he said. Will was not encouraged to write as a child, and he is glad that schools focus on writing more today.

Will does not use email, but you can write to him by sending a letter to his publisher. The address is: Will Hobbs, Author; HarperCollins Books for Young Readers; 1350 Avenue of the Americas; New York, NY 10019.

Will attends book signings for his fans.

All his life, Will has enjoyed wildlife.

WEB LINKS

Will Hobbs' Official Website

www.willhobbsauthor.com

Visit this website to find out more about Will Hobbs and his adventure stories. Click on his stories to find out about how he wrote each book.

The Official Website of Will's Publisher, Harper-Collins

www.harpercollinschildrens.com

Visit this site to find out more about Will's books.

Quiz

Q: What did Will's father do?

1

A: He was an air force engineer.

Q: How many brothers and sisters does Will have?

2

A: Four

3

Q: What were Will's favorite stories as a child?

A: *Treasure Island* was his favorite, although he also really liked *Tom Sawyer*.

Q: What did Will bring to Mr. Pilch's class?

A: A snake for the terrarium

Q: What is the name of the ranch that Will worked at before he went to university?

A: Philmont Scout Ranch in New Mexico

Q: From what university did Will graduate?

A: Will started off at Notre Dame but quickly transferred to Stanford University.

Q: Will stayed home from school to read which books?

A: The Lord of the Rings trilogy

Q: What is Will's wife's name?

A: Jean

Q: What is the name of Will's first published book?

A: *Changes in Latitudes*

Q: How long was Will a teacher?

A: Seventeen years

Writing Terms

This glossary will introduce you to some of the main terms in the field of writing. Understanding these common writing terms will allow you to discuss your ideas about books and writing with others.

action: the moving events of a work of fiction

antagonist: the person in the story who opposes the main character

autobiography: a history of a person's life written by that person

biography: a written account of another person's life

character: a person in a story, poem, or play

climax: the most exciting moment or turning point in a story

episode: a short piece of action, or scene, in a story

fiction: stories about characters and events that are not real

foreshadow: hinting at something that is going to happen later in the book

imagery: a written description of a thing or idea that brings an image to mind

narrator: the speaker of the story who relates the events

nonfiction: writing that deals with real people and events

novel: published writing of considerable length that portrays characters within a story

plot: the order of events in a work of fiction

protagonist: the leading character of a story; often a likable character

resolution: the end of the story, when the conflict is settled

scene: a single episode in a story

setting: the place and time in which a work of fiction occurs

theme: an idea that runs throughout a work of fiction

Glossary

artifacts: objects made or changed by humans, especially tools or weapons used in the past

avid: to do something a lot

backpacking: hiking a long distance, usually with a large backpack

breakthrough: a sudden ability to do something

captive: to hold as a prisoner

devoted: focused all of your attention

draft: a rough copy of something written

experiences: events that someone has lived through

exploring: traveling over an area to find things

inspired: to give a strong feeling to do something

Klondike Gold Rush: about 100,000 people came to Alaska and Canada's Yukon in 1897 and 1898 after gold was discovered there

manuscripts: drafts of a story that is written before it is published

pioneer: someone who explores unknown territory and settles there

procrastinates: puts off doing something

rejection: to send something back that is not wanted

revised: to do something again

scholarship: a financial award to attend school

terrarium: a glass container for plants

transformed: changed into something else

transferred: moved from one place to another

Index

Photo Credits

Every reasonable effort has been made to trace ownership and to obtain permission to reprint copyright material. The publishers would be pleased to have any errors or omissions brought to their attention so that they may be corrected in subsequent printings.

Will Hobbs and Jean Hobbs: pages 1, 3, 4, 7, 8, 9, 10, 11, 12, 13, 16, 17, 22, 23, 26, 27, 28; **Jacket Cover from Downriver by Will Hobbs, copyright © 1992 by Robert McGinnis. Used by permission of Random House Children's Books, a division of Random House, Inc.:** page 21.